Pirates Don't Go To KINDERGARTEN!

By **Lisa Robinson**   Illustrated by **Eda Kaban**

two lions

To Zoe and Naomi and the wonderful preschool teachers who inspired this tale
—L. R.

To my li'l friend Bells
—E. K.

Published by Two Lions, New York

www.apub.com

Amazon, the Amazon logo, and Two Lions are trademarks of
Amazon.com, Inc., or its affiliates.

ISBN-13: 9781542092753 (hardcover)
ISBN-10: 1542092752 (hardcover)

The illustrations are rendered in digital media.

Book design by AndWorld Design
Printed in China

First Edition

10 9 8 7 6 5 4 3 2 1

On the first day of kindergarten,
Emma raided her sea chest.

Treasure map. *Check.*

Spyglass. *Check.*

Cutlass. *Check.*

She was ready to set sail.

If only Cap'n Chu—the roughest, toughest, awesomest preschool pirate cap'n ever—
could see her now.

After a stormy crossing,
Emma finally dropped anchor at school.
She scanned her treasure map.

"Kindergarten, ho!"

But instead of boarding the kindergarten ship . . .

. . . she sailed into preschool.
"Ahoy, Cap'n Chu!" Emma hollered.

"Ahoy! Good to see you, Emma," said Ms. Chu.
"But the kindergarten classroom's down the hall."

Emma peered through her spyglass.

Wrong classroom.
Wrong cubbies.
Wrong toys.

Worst of all—wrong captain.

"Pirates don't go to kindergarten!" said Emma.

"Ocean's rough today!" said Cap'n Chu.
"Batten down the hatches, mateys.
I'm rowing this sailor to her new ship."

"Emma, meet Cap'n Hayes.
She's in charge of this spaceship."

"Welcome. You're just in time for liftoff!"
said Ms. Hayes.

Emma leaped onto the gangway and stared through the hatch.

Stars?

Planets?

Rocket ships?

It wasn't the high seas, but maybe with a few changes here and there it could work. . . .

But a new captain?

NO!

"**Arrrrr**," Emma growled. "You'll never take me alive!"

SPLASH!

Emma swam back to Cap'n Chu's ship.

THUMP!
CLUMP!

She stomped her peg leg.

SCRUNCH!
SPLAT!

She dug for doubloons and scattered sand.

"Yo ho ho!" she sang at the top of her lungs.

"Pirate Emma! You know the rules," Ms. Chu said.
"No throwing sand, and use your inside voice, please."

"PIRATES
DON'T
FOLLOW
RULES!"

A kindergartner poked her head through a porthole.

"Ms. Hayes needs a hand feeding the guinea pig.
Can Emma come?"

"Hi, Daniela," said Ms. Chu.
"Emma, they need your help on the other ship."

"A guinea pig in need?!
Aye, aye, Cap'n!"

Back at the kindergarten spaceship, Daniela gave Emma a tour. She introduced Emma to lots of busy astronauts before taking her to see some special cargo.

"Say hello to our guinea pig, Betty."

"**Blimey!** She's a pirate pig. I'm going to call her Beastly Betty."

After she snuggled and fed the pirate pig, Emma inspected the kindergarten spaceship.

There was a nature center— but no Cap'n Chu to look at seeds with;

an art studio— but no Cap'n Chu to show her paintings to;

a reading nook—
but no Cap'n Chu to
read books to her.

There were even some astronauts doing experiments
at a science station—

BUT STILL NO CAP'N CHU!

"Pirates don't feed pigs!"

SPLASH!

Emma swam back to Cap'n Chu's ship.

Emma mustered some mates and seized control of the preschool ship.

"MUTINY!"

The pirate band sneered and snarled,
whooped and hollered,
raced up the rigging,
and climbed to the crow's nest.

"I've come to parley," said Ms. Chu.
"How do I get my ship back?"

"Come with me to kindergarten!"

"But I have to lead this new band of pirates."

"THEN WALK THE PLANK!"
Emma brandished her cutlass.
"Tie her up, mates."

"It's time to join your new mates!" Ms. Chu said.

"Kindergarten looks like fun," Emma whispered. "But I won't sail with a new captain."

"Shiver me timbers, Peg Leg Emma! Cap'n Hayes is the finest cap'n in the universe."

Emma slid closer. "**But she's not . . . you.**"

"I'll miss you, too." Ms. Chu hugged Emma.

"Can pirates visit their old captain? And borrow her bandanna?"

"Of course."

Ms. Hayes rowed into the room.

"We're short one crew member for our spaceship. Can you spare someone brave and strong? Like Emma?"

Emma swam away from Cap'n Chu's ship.

SPLASH!

"Open the shuttle hatch."

"Pirates do go to kindergarten!"